Temptation has never been so sweet...

Richard Martin's life was only just starting to come back together, then
she opened the door in that damn little black robe that shows off plenty
of leg, and every curve.
She, Rebecca Blaire, the girl from downstairs. His babysitter.
She's everyman's fantasy, a big doe-eyed nymph, as beautiful as she is
innocent.
Forbidden fruit in every sense of the word.
And she desperately needs his help, before her abusive father comes
home and beats her black and blue.
Richard knew he should just walk away. It wasn't any of his business
really, and nothing good could come from going through that door, but
then...
Some temptations are just too sweet to resist.

*Sweet Temptations: The Babysitter is the original debut from the
Lord of Lust, L.M. Mountford, a sizzling tale of lust and temptation
that will ignite your ereader and leave you panting for more as it
follows a modern man's journey across the Rubicon.
With all the heat of Sylvia Day but only some of the drama of Bridget
Jones, Sweet Temptations is one you don't want to miss. This new
edition includes a sneak peek of its long-awaited sequel, The Boss's
Daughter.*

Sweet Temptations: Babysitter

L.M. Mountford

L.M. Mountford -- 1st Ed.
ISBN: 978-1-913945-29-9

About The Author

L.M. Mountford's goal in life is to be unique, a character who stands out from the crowd that you just can't help remembering with a bemused chuckle.

A born and bred country boy from the southwest of England, he knew from an early age that he wanted to write and spent most of his time writing story ideas or playing Star Wars on his PlayStation.

Not much has changed over the years, though his stories have grown decidedly dirtier, and he swapped the Star Wars for Call of Duty.

Dubbed the Lord of Lust in 2019 and a firm believer that nothing sells like sex and violence, he loves writing about hard and gritty romantic thrillers, loaded with action men, sassy heroines, and a whole lot of dirty, sexy heat.

Sign up for L.M. Mountford's VIP newsletter to details of free books, new releases, discounts, ARC opportunities AND receive a FREE steamy read.

Form available on **LMMountford.com**

L.M
Mountford
The Lost

Bibliography

For a complete reading list, visit LMMountford.com/bibliography/

Collections
Deliciously Sinful Liaisons
Sweet Temptations Box Set
Romancing the Tropics
Just a Number
The Sweet Temptations Series
The Babysitter
The Boss's Daughter
Just Friends Series
Just Once
Broken Heart Series
Broken
Tropical Cocktail Romance
Tequila Sunset
Beneath the Sheets
Confessions of a Trophy Wife
Forbidden Desire
Rogue Warrior
Rogue
Stand-alone Titles
Uncovered
Serving the Senator
Reckless
Training Tracey

Sweet Temptations

LM
Mountford

Sweet Temptations

THE LORD OF LUST

L.M. MOUNTFORD

Chapter One

Richard Martin always hated Holmes & Raine's Christmas parties. The décor reminded him of a cheap Hammer Horror set. The atmosphere was reminiscent of a funeral. And worst of all, they were organised in August and hosted in early November.

Each year, the bosses would present a laundry list of reasons for the premature celebration, but everyone knew those were merely a smokescreen, devised to mask the fact that it cost considerably less to hold a Christmas party before December. Frankly, Richard wondered why they bothered even holding a party, or, for that matter, made attendance mandatory.

Subtly pushing up his left sleeve cuff, he checked his watch for what felt like the hundredth time. To his utter disgust, the digital display indicated that it was just *10:03 pm*.

The *party* would go on for at least another hour, maybe even two, God forbid!

The dining hall of the Cheltenham Premier Inn was a hive of colour and light as the *value* disco ball fitted to the ceiling pelted the chamber with light beams and the speakers blared out a stream of Christmas hits from the 90s. The walls were decorated in red and white. Mistletoe hung on strands of crimson silk, and an artificial Christmas tree stood in the centre of the room beside a folding table heavily laden with snacks and refreshments. The guests appeared jubilant and festive as they revelled in small groups evenly spaced around the cavernous chamber, mirroring the groups that clung together around the office's coffee and tea machines. They were garbed elegantly in suits and dresses, a façade of wealth and importance that was as phoney as their smiling faces. God, he needed a drink.

Resisting the urge to check his watch, Richard got up from his assigned seat and moved into the crowd, the wooden soles of his shoes clapping loudly on the tiles as he weaved a path between the mingling bodies, nodding politely at anyone who noticed him, towards the overloaded folding table. There were ample snacks and refreshments, Asda's finest. Diced sausage rolls, cocktail sausages, crisps, biscuits, fruit and cheese on cocktail sticks, mini-pizzas, and even some slices of chocolate sponge, all laid out in white china bowls and saucers around two large bottles of Jacob's Creek and Honeyed Jack Daniel's, as well as a jug of iced orange squash. Two high towers of Styrofoam cups had been erected between the bottles.

Taking the cup on the top of the tower, he contemplated the wine for a moment, tempted to pour a drink, but then thought better of it. Alice would kill him if she found out. Grumbling inwardly, he mournfully poured himself a squash. The wine was probably vinegar anyway, he reasoned, before twisting to take another look around the room while sipping the fruity beverage.

He glimpsed Stacy Stevens, a pretty part-timer, in the firm's mailroom with long raven black hair and milky skin, nervously edging through the crowd in her black lacy dress and flat-bottomed shoes; somehow seeming even more uncomfortable than him amongst the revellers. Nearby, he saw Mark McClaine, his office colleague and friend, and his wife Rachael deep in conversation with another couple he didn't recognise. And deepest amidst the denizens, the firm's MD, Derik Holmes, was conversing with the heads of departments and grinning broadly as he took long swigs from a monogrammed silver and crocodile-leather hip flask. Silver-haired, rosy-faced, and with the frame of a barrel wrapped in Armani, Derik was the very embodiment of opulent living and Richard could only hope the man didn't notice him for he was awfully fond of mocking and belittling anyone whom he considered beneath him. Fortunately, the four department heads seemed to be commanding the full wrath of the Director's humour and he failed to notice the lowly bookkeeper standing beside the refreshments. Alas, there was no sign of Alice amidst the sea of faces, but neither, thankfully, could he see…

"Well, well, well, look who we have here?" an all too familiar voice said silkily.

Fuck. Throwing his head back, Richard drained the cup in a single swig before placing it back on the table and turning, slowly, around to be confronted by the vision of his supervisor, Scarlet Holmes, standing before him. Strikingly beautiful with soft features and sun-kissed skin, her hair was long, wavy tresses of honey blonde that reached down to her shoulders. Clad in a dark blue pencil dress that went well with her almost unnaturally bright baby blue eyes and clung to her slender figure, the low-cut V-neckline offering a tantalising glimpse of her ample cleavage, she would have seemed utterly radiant if he hadn't known the beauty was only skin deep.

"Hi Scarlet," he said nervously before flashing her a smile he was certain Stevie Wonder would have seen through; "enjoying the party?"

"Mmm…" she purred, watching him with a wicked amusement that Richard wasn't sure he liked. Then again, he rarely knew how to feel around Scarlet Holmes. Though she'd only been twenty-three and barely out of University when she joined the firm, she was also the CEO's daughter and had leapt over the heads of a dozen more highly qualified employees to get the Accounting Supervisor's position. What made it all the worse was, unlike the stereotypical cliché of a ditzy boss's daughter, Scarlet actually knew her trade. Despite having an attitude that constantly swung from aggressive to flirtatious, she had a genuine business acumen as well as a knack for people and figures. She was ambitious and worked tirelessly to ensure that she and her people regularly went above and beyond. Thanks largely to her efforts, they were now the top performing team in the firm and rumour had it, she was about to be promoted to the Head of the Accounts Department. However, there were also whispers. Rumour had it that she'd had numerous affairs with more than half the firm's employees, many of whom were happily married. For his part, Richard preferred not to put stock in the storm of office gossip that followed where ever she went, but in one thing, at least, the rumours were true. She was a real tight arse. "Where's your wife? I haven't seen her. Is everything alright between you two?"

"Oh…" His eyes flickered towards the door leading out of the hall to the building's main foyer, hoping against hope to see his wife sashaying towards them. "Alice just stepped out for a minute. She had to take a call but couldn't hear herself over the music." His tongue darted out to moisten his dry lips. "She should be back any minute now." And he hoped that was true. The words sounded hollow to his ears, sounding foreign and unfamiliar and he suddenly had the feeling of being trapped as he realised just how close they were, her curvaceous body all but pinning him against the table. "So-so, how's your father? He looks like he's…enjoying himself."

He gestured with a nod over her shoulder and Scarlet twisted to a look back across the hall to where her father was telling a very animated story. At the sight of a short and portly man with thinning red-grey hair Richard had seen around the office a few times but had never been introduced to, standing a few paces away, she made only a token effort to cover her laugh with a cough. With a face such a deep shade of red it was almost purple and watching the inside of his cup so intently, clearly determined to look anywhere but at his immediate superior, the tomfoolery could only have been at his expense.

"Well, you know Daddy, always happy so long as there is a drink in his glass and minions to torment." It was meant as a joke and Richard tried to match her gleeful chuckle, but his heart just wasn't in it and he could tell she saw through the façade. Suddenly, her playfulness evaporated.

When she turned back, the stern mask that so often watched him like a hawk whenever he handed in his reports suddenly glared up at him with eyes as cold and hard as diamonds. The shift was so abrupt it almost gave him vertigo. "He has his eye on you."

"Me?" Swallowing the knot suddenly rising in his throat, he forced himself to hold her gaze, fighting the impulse to glance towards the Director. The urge was like burning fishing lures hooked into his eyes, tugging insistently, and he fully expected to spy the Managing Director shooting him a glare, the mirror image of his daughter's. But why? What the hell would walrus face want with him?

"The Prometheus Account." Scarlet supplied by way of explanation, arching one perfectly plucked eyebrow. Full pink lips pulled tight into an almost indefinable line.

Prometheus was a London based construction and land developments company that had several branches throughout the continent and, according to their books, also had contracts in parts of Central America, Asia, Africa and the Middle East. Though it was not exactly an uncommon practice for big organisations to outsource their accounts, indeed Holmes & Raine had more than a dozen such contracts, there was no question that the Prometheus Account was a big deal. Rumour had it that Derik Holmes had superseded two department heads to ensure his daughter received the account. With explicit instructions, it was to be given top priority. Whether that was true or not, she, in turn, had called Richard into her office and instructed him to delegate his workload around the rest of the team. She wanted Prometheus to be his sole concern. Everything else was to go on the back burner. So he had.

She'd also told him to have it done ASAP. That had been three weeks ago, and the reports were still stashed on the flash drive he kept locked away in his desk drawer.

"Ahhh…" He swallowed, the knot in his stomach leaping sickeningly into his throat. He should have known. Hell, he should have given her the damn USB last week. Withholding it had been stupid.

For all the weight laid on his shoulders, it hadn't taken him long at all to sort and organise and check Prometheus' accounts. It was such easy work; a trained chimp would have been up to the task. Their records were meticulous and immaculate. The numbers perfect. And, what with the pressure to finish the job, the importance of the contract to the company and the fact his performance review was upcoming; withholding the data was more trouble than his job's worth. Withholding it had been very stupid, but Richard couldn't help himself. In his twelve years in accounting, he had never seen anything like it, and that irked him. He couldn't put his finger on what, the numbers were just…too perfect. Or too perfect to be genuine.

Of course, it wasn't any concern of his. He wasn't an analyst. It wasn't his job to sort out conundrums. He just kept the client's books. When he was done, he sent reports to Scarlet with notes about his concerns and recommendations, if any; but in this, he couldn't help himself.

It almost felt like there was a challenge hidden amidst the sheer mass of paper and data, of piles of receipts, invoices and spreadsheets. Something secret only he could see. Hidden, waiting, daring him to find it. So, he'd begun to dig, looking deeper, trying to solve a mystery that common sense screamed didn't exist, but that the small voice in the back of his mind refused to let go, like some naughty schoolboy playing truant to go on a great adventure in the land of Narnia.

Sooner or later though, the boy needed to go back through the wardrobe, and if the Managing Director had his eye on Richard... So far, every money trail had turned up empty and by itself, mere professional curiosity wasn't worth losing a job over. Or, worse still, becoming the next punchline in one of walrus face's jokes.

Baleful blue eyes glared up at him, chunks of blue ice burning bright against a sea of soft beauty. Richard forced a small, reassuring smile. "I'll have them on your desk Monday.

"Good" That single word was like a storm passing to unveil sunbursts. She beamed with the radiance, her golden skin lighting up with a warmth that chased any hint of chill away as those luscious pink lips curled into a smile. "See that you do, or else I might just have to give you a spanking." She winked.

Richard gawped, not sure whether to believe his own ears. Had she really just said that?

To anyone who might have glanced their way, the gesture would have appeared innocent. Yet her eyes lost none of their intensity as she watched him, and her playful tone sent a warm, involuntary shiver coursing up his spine. What the fuck?

He remembered all the stories he'd heard people at work gossiping about the people who'd told them and the wide range of vague, outlandish details that seemed to grow more and more extraordinary with each retelling. It was all hearsay. Mostly just the petty vindictiveness of someone who'd been put out, or thought her job should have been theirs, or just the usual rambling talk that always seemed to blossom around a famous name. There had never been any proof, and until now, Richard had barely given them much thought. But that look in her eyes made him ready to believe every word. He'd seen it on the cats he sometimes saw stalking city streets on his morning drive to work. There was the same confidence, the same purpose and… hunger.

She watched him the way a stalking cat would observe a bird pecking in the mud, utterly fixed in its own world and ripe for the plucking, and the thought had him instinctively averting his gaze. Whatever this game was, he didn't want a part of it. However, knowing she was waiting for him to say something, he opened his mouth to agree but the words that should have come caught in his throat and all he could do was nod in acknowledgement. Heat blossoming across his cheeks, he swallowed, his mouth so dry it felt like forcing down a lemon. Goddamnit, he needed a drink.

Her eyes flashed, victorious fire dancing over cool blue ice. Then, as if only just realising she was making him uncomfortable, her smile faltered for a moment and turned apologetic. "Awww don't worry, Dick. I was only kidding," she cooed like he was a small child or pet dog. "I think you better have another drink. If your face gets any redder, they might mistake you for Rudolph and hang you on the wall." She giggled, the sound all girlish and mocking. "It's already a rather striking likeness. Maybe with a pair of antlers-"

More relieved than embarrassed by her dismissal, Richard turned back to the refreshments before Scarlet had finished speaking. With the Styrofoam cup still in hand and grateful for some much-needed space between him and the teasing wench, he reached out for the jug of squash. To his horror, the hand was shaking. No! God, get a grip man. Don't let her get to you.

As if she knew his thoughts, Scarlet stepped in close enough for him to inhale her perfume. Something sharp and expensive.

"Here, let me," she offered. Brushing his hand aside, she seized the handle and, despite it being almost full, raised the jug one-handed. With a slight pivot of her hips to face him, she filled his cup almost all the way to the top, her gaze unwavering, boring into his with that look of predatory glee, seeing through him, into him. It was unnervingly similar to the look Alice shot him whenever she suspected he was up to something. "There." She put the jug down before finally breaking the contact to give the drink a quizzical look. "Just orange? You don't want to mix it with something a little stronger?"

"N-no thanks. I'm driving." Barely able to get his tongue around the words, Richard had to fight the urge to immediately knock the drink back. Fuck, where the hell was Alice? What could Samantha have to say that couldn't wait for tomorrow? He looked down at the orange in his cup, wished, though he'd never been much of a drinker, that it could be something fermented, and added under his breath without thinking, "Alice would kick my arse if she found out I'd been drinking." The moment he'd said them, he regretted the words. Beaten, he surrendered and chucked the juice back in almost one big gulp. It was deliciously refreshing and eased the knots in his gut in a single rush of watered citrus.

"Ohhh…" Mirth lit up Scarlet's eyes. "Well, isn't someone a slave driver. Come on, Dick, I promise I won't tell…" she teased, playfully reaching for the Honeyed Jack Daniel's. Richard struggled not to grin at the impish mischief on her face.

"No, it's fine, I don't really like mixing drinks anyway."

She feigned a pout that had no doubt melted her daddy's heart more than once. It had the effect of making her look so serenely demure and girlish. He might have been convinced she was sincere if not for that wild glint in her eyes. It was a sinful look on her, the perfect melding of innocent and wicked. All that was missing was an Anne Summers costume, probably a nurse or cheerleader's uniform.

A shiver coursed up at his spine at the thought of Scarlet in such a skimpy ensemble. Her long legs encased in knee socks and vanishing into a miniskirt that seemed to promise a glimpse of whatever she had on, or not, underneath with every movement. A tight-fitting crop top stretched tight over her full breasts but cut just short enough to show off her flat stomach. Golden hair bouncing in pigtails as she played with a set of pom-poms…

Richard mentally shook himself, trying to clear the image. He wasn't a horny teen anymore. Those sorts of thoughts were trouble. He was married. And she was his boss. Off limits didn't even begin to cover it. However, his body apparently disagreed and, to his horror, the image roused a very vital part of his anatomy into life. Registering the stirring, he instinctively glanced down to see an already visible bulge rising against his left trouser leg. He shifted, trying to cover his visibly straining erection before glancing back up. But Scarlet must have already noticed because the pouting girl was gone. Instead, she was grinning toothily, her eyes bright. Pink tongue darting out to slowly moisten her full kissable lips, she mouthed "busted."

Time held its breath. Somewhere in the hall, a guffaw rang out. The timing was purely coincidental, but even still the humiliation hit him like a bucket of ice water. Dammit, what the fuck was going on? He couldn't believe this was happening. He needed to think, to get some air before this got any worse and his boss decided to whip out her phone to immortalise the moment.

Contrary to being impeded, however, the realisation he'd been caught only had Richard's cock stiffening to full mast against its confinement. To his enormous relief, no one else appeared to notice.

Scarlet's eyes widened, her smile faltering to form a perfect 'O'. "Oh… my!"

Well-aware of what had caught her attention, Richard turned his eyes up to the hall's plain white ceiling and ornamental brass chandelier-style lights draped with tinsel, desperate to look at something, anything, but the woman eyeing his dick. To his enormous relief, no one else appeared to have noticed. He felt like a little Robin red breast that had spotted a cat stalking it in the grass and taken flight, rising high on a wing of elation and the adrenaline of escaping death. Only to be swatted from the sky and brought crashing back down, its last moment consumed by the image of the sleek feline body arching into the sky, hooked claws reaching out and fangs bared. I tawt I taw a puddy tat, indeed.

"Have you heard anything about your promotion?" he asked without thinking, studying the interlaced webs of gold, red and green tinsel that enveloped the nearest light.

"Y-yes…" For all her customary swagger, the silky soft voice sounded breathless and the shaky timbre drew his gaze irresistibly back to her. Scarlet glared back at him. Her eyes narrowed and cheeks tinged a faint shade of pink. She seemed to be musing about whether to say more, searching for a trap behind the question, and the uncertainty reflected in those bright blue irises had him blowing out a slow breath that released all the tension from his body.

Scarlet obviously sensed, or noticed, the change in him, however, because the gleam of predatory amusement returned to her eyes. She'd play whatever game he had in mind, and she'd play to win. "Daddy says the job's mine if I want it, but first I need to get my house in order. He's starting to think we might have a loose cannon on deck." She leant casually back against the refreshments table with her hands gripping the edges to distribute her weight and back, curving just enough to emphasise her breasts. It was a pose that would have put many magazine centrefolds to shame. "But let's not talk shop. This is a party, after all. How is your son, Alex, isn't it? I saw the pictures on your desk. He must be nearly two now?"

Richard held her gaze, refusing to take the bait even as his eyes were instinctively drawn to the slopes of her breasts. "Almost sixteen months, yes." He swallowed, a bitter taste rising in the back of his throat, not liking the way this conversation was turning. "And he's fine, hasn't quite got the hang of walking yet. Can't quite find his feet, so he's always losing his balance mid-step. We've had a lot of scuffs and tears, but he keeps getting back up." He couldn't quite keep the pride from his voice. So many kids would burst into a fit of tears whenever they fell over and refuse to move until their parents picked them up, but Alex never stopped. Even in tears, he would push himself up and keep crawling to where he wanted to go.

"And you and Alice are coping well?" she asked, cocking her head to the side. A curl of locks fell out of place, but Scarlet didn't brush it aside, her eyes searching his. "I doubt it could have been easy starting a family so soon after losing your job. Your career taking such a huge step back and having to pack up your lives to move here. Not many marriages could weather the storm so well. Maybe you two should write one of those self-help books. Money woes and job lows - A couple's survival guide." She chuckled, the sound dry and mocking.

Forcing a small smile, Richard resisted the impulse to give her the finger. I prefer Don't Let the Tarts Get You Down. "We're Fine." Of course, it was a half-truth. They fought, sometimes like cats and dogs, over nothing at all, and other times they fought to avoid the very real issues looming over them. There had been many of those recently, but he wasn't about to discuss that with Scarlet.

"I see." With that, she pushed away from the table and fingered the stray lock of hair back behind her ear. "Tell me, Dick, would you consider it cheating to kiss me under the mistletoe?" She said it casually, as if it was as every day as asking about the weather.

Already on edge and walking on eggshells, the broadside caught Richard completely by surprise and had him almost doubling over in a fit of dry, heaving coughs so violent it was a marvel he didn't choke. "Ex-ex-excuse me?" he stammered, certain he must have misheard her.

Smiling teasingly, she stepped closer so that as she looked up; they were almost nose-to-nose. "It was a perfectly simple question." A hand tipped by baby blue nails reached out, taking the cup from his grasp and placing it on the refreshment table before tracing her finger up along the lapel of his jacket and along the line of his jaw. "Would you consider kissing another woman under the mistletoe as being unfaithful to your wife?"

Her eyes flickered to the ceiling overhead and, pressing firmly on his chin, she tilted his head back. Too stunned to resist, he followed her gaze skyward to where three leaves of mistletoe were hanging off a scrap of crimson silk dangling above their heads.

Richard's chest constricted. "I...I..."

"Cat got your tongue?"

Richard wheeled, the pit falling out of his stomach as the all too familiar voice asked and brought a frosty blast of reality. Alice Serena Martin stood not three steps away with her arms crossed and glaring at her husband. "Am I interrupting something?" she asked icily.

"Darling," Richard tried to make the greeting sound reassuring, but the rush of fear and arousal the sight of her provoked in him at that moment made it hard to do anything. Even after all the years they'd been married, the sight of her could still leave him speechless. Pale as milk and utterly gorgeous, she wore only the smallest amount of makeup and a sultry, backless evening gown of black satin that moulded perfectly to her hourglass figure. A slit from thigh to hem flashed a glimpse of smooth, flawlessly toned legs that seemed to go forever as she walked. Though shorter than most, her tiny stature barely scraping five feet when propped up by the stilettos she'd worn for the party, his wife was a downright knockout with her sharp, pronounced bone structure, hair that ran down her back in a long wash of silken mahogany, and intense grey-blue eyes.

Yet now her beauty had been contorted into a twisted mask that gave her the hard face of a hawk. Eyes that had stared up at him with such love and devotion, now piercing with accusation. That look cut deeper than steel. He wanted to say something to reassure her, but, somehow, a line like 'it's not what it looks like' just didn't seem it.

"Ahh, Alice!" Scarlet stepped around Richard, into the older woman's sights. She beamed, her eyes alight with wicked delight. "There you are. We were just talking about you."

Alice's cool gaze shifted to the blonde, her lips pursing into a fine line "Indeed."

"In fact, *Dick* was just telling me about your son. He's such a handsome little boy, you must be very proud.

"Yes."

Scarlet gave Richard a slow, appraising look, then smiled knowingly. "He's the spitting image of his father. Good luck keeping the girls away. You'll have to beat them off with a big pole." Dread's cold fingers crept down Richard's spine at Scarlet's added emphasis. Dammit, was she going to try and start a fight?

Though the women had only met on a handful of occasions, exchanging barely more than a handful of words each time, for whatever instinctive, irrational reason, the atmosphere had crackled around them. He could feel it building, raising the hairs on the back of his neck, and knew that rather than finding salvation in his wife, he'd jumped straight out of the frying pan, into the fire.

"Well, I'll manage." Missing nothing, Alice's gaze narrowed momentarily on her husband, who couldn't help shifting guiltily on the balls of his feet under the hawk-like stare, before returning to the younger woman. "But I'm sure you can give me a few pointers sometime. *Dick* tells me you've handled lots of woodwork around the firm." She forced a wry smile. Richard, of course, had never said anything of the sort, but he wasn't about to contradict her. "Your father must be very proud that you're treating his staff so well after he gave you a job?"

For all of a moment, Scarlet's eyes widened in surprise. Then she recovered her composure and her smile melted away into a small, derisive twist. "What can I say? I like to keep the men under me satisfied. Dick's never has any complaints." Alice's nostrils flared and the fingers that had been creeping down Richard's spine closed around his gut, but Scarlet appeared not to notice. She shrugged, her eyes trailing over Alice from head to toe, scrutinising her like she would a document that came across her desk. "That's such a lovely dress, Alice. Is it new?"

Oh, fuck! Richard didn't need to look at his wife to know that, if Scarlet was trying to pick a fight, then she'd just hit her mark. He knew he should step in, but Alice shot a look that warned him to stay out of it. The corner of her lip rose just enough to reveal the glint of white teeth, something she only did when she meant business and had him glancing nervously around the room.

Fortunately, no one seemed interested in taking advantage of the buffet or paying the confrontation any notice, yet.

"You deserve to treat yourself." Scarlet pushed on, her voice laced with a sympathetic tone that was all pity and mocking. "Was it hard to find one in your new size? It would be just awful after you worked so hard to shed the last of that pesky baby weight, but I guess some things just can't be helped..."

Alright, he needed to put an end to this. Whatever Scarlet's game was, she had gone over the line.

Like so many women, Alice had always been overly self-conscious of her appearance. While no one could ever accuse his 110-pound wife, who could put away a whole pizza like Richard did a good 18oz steak, of being anorexic, she was borderline obsessive about her weight. One of her main requirements, when they'd been flat hunting, was that there had to be a nearby gym, and she visited it almost daily. After Alex was born, she'd worked hard to rid herself of the pregnancy pounds and even harder now to maintain her figure. She would give back as good as she got and believed in taking the bull by the horns. If a child tried to fob off not doing their homework, she called them on it. When something went wrong at home and he wasn't in, she dealt with it.

So, if Scarlet wanted a fight, Alice would damn well give her one. Even if that was exactly what the little strumpet was counting on.

Richard opened his mouth to intervene, not at all interested in finding out just what his wife might say, or do for that matter, with so many people around them. Only Scarlet rounded on him before he could get a word out. Her eyes were bright with an impish mischief that made him want to run a hand through his hair.

"Anyway." She cocked her head as if remembering an afterthought, her hair tumbling over one shoulder and exposing the long slope of her neck, as well as giving him a glimpse down the valley of her breasts. "I just so happened to notice that piece of mistletoe hanging up there. So, I asked *Dickie* if he considers it being unfaithful to kiss me." She slid forward a step. Heat bristled across the back of Richard's neck, the fury in Alice's stare burning his skin as Scarlet pressed into him and touched a hand to his cheek before he could think to pull away. The closeness as intoxicating as the perfume suddenly fogging his thoughts and her eyes held his. "It's such a small tradition I know, but they say it's bad luck to ignore it."

"Ohhh really?" Alice shouldered past the younger woman. Scarlet reeled, almost sprawling to the floor, before catching her balance at the last moment. "Then allow me." Her hands tangled in husband's hair, fisting and dragging his head down so their lips crashed together in a fierce kiss.

The sudden embrace stole his breath away and he couldn't help uttering a ragged moan as her tongue forced its way past his lips to meet his in a feverish dance. His hands rose on their own accord to circle around her waist before trailing down her back to grasp her full buttocks, roughly pulling her against him and drawing a low moan from his wife. Then, just as quickly as she had begun, Alice broke the kiss and drew away from the embrace. Short of breath, Richard could only grin down at his wife's satisfied smirk.

"Yea! Get in there, Richard, my son!" Mark called, followed by a sudden uproar of applause and catcalls as every face in the hall zeroed in on them. Breathing hard,

Richard forced a smile and raised a hand in thanks, only to be elbowed in the ribs by the equally embarrassed Alice.

"Geez, get a room." Scarlet snarled, her smirk replaced by a scowl. "Maybe you should go before they demand an encore. See you on Monday, *Dick*." Then, starting to worry her bottom lip, she turned on her heel. "Nice to see you again Alice."

"Bitch," Alice cursed under her breath, watching the younger woman's retreating figure with a look of utter malice, before taking her husband's hand in hers and dragging him through the mass of clapping hands and out of the two huge glass doors that opened out onto the Premier Inn's rear garden. It was a cold night, even for mid-November, and the cloudless canopy above twinkled with stars that lit the ground just enough for them to make out the cobbled path leading around the structure to the car park. A frigid wind whistled by and Richard hesitated, remembering that Alice hadn't been wearing a jacket, but she dragged him along. Though wearing five-inch heels, she traversed the tricky stones with ease while he was left almost tumbling over his own feet to keep up with her.

Polished and gleaming, their immaculate black Volkswagen Golf would have been almost invisible in the hotel's car park if not for the solitary lamppost standing sentinel, bathing the vehicle in golden light. Unlocking it with a quick press on the key in his pocket, he held the passenger side door open for his wife to enter the vehicle before closing it and moving around to get in the driver's side. However, no sooner had he pushed the key into the ignition did Alice round on him.

"So, what really happened between you and that tart, Scarlet?" she hissed, seething like a cobra in her venom.

"What? Nothing…. nothing at all…" Richard gasped, shooting her an uneasy smile that he prayed she might find convincing. Her stern look promised otherwise, however, and he quickly turned back to the windscreen, a heavy sigh passing his lips as he fastened his seatbelt and activated the dipped headlights. "Really… it was nothing; she was just asking me a question about mistletoe. And that's all." Twisting the key, he let the engine roar to life and then reversed out of the space before shifting into gear and driving from the car park out onto Gloucester Road.

"Ohhh really…*Dick?*" she spat accusingly, the nickname rolling off her tongue as a long serpentine hiss.

"Ugh! Bloody hell, Alice, this is ridiculous!" he growled, tearing his eyes off the road for a moment to shoot her a reproachful glare. Fortunately, there was little traffic, and the Golf purred like a kitten as they sped along the deserted dual carriageway, angrily challenging every traffic light at a steady 60mph. Yet when a metallic blue Vauxhall convertible roared out of the darkness, overtaking them with a sound like a thunderclap, he couldn't resist the challenge and sped after it. Flooring it, he'd caught up to the sleek two-seater in a matter of seconds, but at a glance from Alice, he eased off the throttle. "Look, I swear, nothing is going on between Scarlet and me."

She watched him suspiciously for a moment more before finally relaxing into her seat, yet he knew she wasn't convinced. Alice was anything but a fool; she'd heard the whispers about his supervisor and, like any good loving wife, she was concerned.

They'd first met fifteen years ago at the University of Bristol. She'd been a 'fresher' studying English literature and out with her *BFFs* on a Saturday night. He'd been a struggling second-year Business Studies student working a double shift in the popular student bar, The Burning Book. While he'd been on the taps, she'd ordered a round of Bloody Marys and when she paid, had handed him a £20 note and a napkin with her mobile number scribbled down. She'd been the first girl to show any real interest in him and, utterly bedazzled by the petite stunner, he'd called her immediately after his shift. Five years later, they were both graduates with promising careers. Alice an English teacher in a prestigious secondary school, him a junior banker. They were also newlyweds, young and in love.

For the first few years of their life as husband and wife, they'd rented a comfortable little flat well within walking distance of Bristol's city centre. However, disaster struck in 2004 when his bank was bought out and amidst the fallout, Richard had lost his job. For the following year they'd lived on a blend of his savings and Alice's salary while he looked for work in the city, but the economic devastation of the recession had left him floundering in a raging river of unemployment and without their prosperous joint income, they'd been forced to move to the smaller, *cheaper*, city of Gloucester.

Feeling the tension hanging between them like a great steel-ball and collar as they left the lights of Cheltenham in their wake and sped down the black stretch of road, Richard changed the subject. "What did Samantha have to say?" Samantha Swift was Alice's oldest and dearest friend, as well as her maid of honour at their wedding. "Shouldn't she be attending to her latest husband's bank balance? Or has the Internet finally run out of shoes and gold?" Alas, the joke fell on deaf ears.

"She's getting divorced."

"What?" He shot her a disbelieving sideways glance. "The ink on her marriage certificate hasn't even dried yet, and she's getting divorced. What happened? Did she bleed the poor bastard dry already? They've only been married a few months."

Growing angry, Alice glared back at him. "No, this time it's different. She caught him in the hot tub with their dog walker." *Damn.*

Feeling his cheeks burn with embarrassment, Richard kept his gaze rooted to the road ahead. Road signs indicated a roundabout half a mile ahead and beyond that, the horizon burned with golden radiance. *Home sweet home.*

Founded at the dawn of the first century AD, on the order of Roman Emperor Nerva and the pride of the Mercian King Æthelred, Gloucester was built along the banks of the River Severn, close to the Welsh border. Though primarily an industrial mecca, the city was a wealth of history and culture, with Tudor architecture still adorning its central streets and the fabled cathedral at its heart.

They drove in silence for several long moments, street lamps bathing them in warm light as they entered the city area. Cruising down Eastern-Avenue past rows of warehouse stores that lined either side, he glimpsed two sets of traffic lights changing from emerald, to amber, to crimson, and began to brake. Downshifting gears, he quickly floored it as the lights changed back just before they came to a complete stop. There were two more sets of lights, but both stayed green as they approached and passed. Despite it being ten-thirty on a Saturday night, the roads were dead and deserted but for the odd cyclist. Houses sprung like weeds as they drove around a roundabout, past a Tesco's garage and took the last exit of an even larger roundabout, capped by a grass isle in its centre. There the road became thin and narrow, winding round numerous snaking twists and flanked with rows of two-storied brick houses on either side, passing a cemetery and an old primary school encircled by high iron spear fencing.

"She's moving into her parents' house on Friday," Alice announced suddenly as they swerved off the main road after passing an ancient church. "I told her you'd be happy to help." She glared at him venomously, as if daring him to refuse.

Steering the vehicle into their parking space, Richard took the car out of gear and put the handbrake on. Taking the key out of the ignition, he turned to his wife, gave her a genuine smile, and said, "Anything for you."

Leaning forward, he seized her lips in a passionate kiss.

Chapter Two

Though the living room door was shut, Richard could dimly hear a movie playing as he shut the front door behind him and Alice. Recognising the cheesy dialogue, he couldn't help but groan in disappointment. *Oh God, please no, not Twilight again!*

The flat was a huge leap down from the one they'd had in Bristol. On the third floor of a five-storey tower block, it had two small bedrooms, one bathroom, and boasted views overlooking Gloucester Park as well as a security door and parking. The rent was also cheap because the flat was on the less desirable side of town.

Slipping off her shoes, Alice went ahead of him and vanished through the wide archway on their right into the kitchen to make a cup of tea whilst he moved down the darkened foyer towards the living room's closed door. "Hey Rebecca, we're home."

A startled gasp and hurried footfalls sounded in answer, and the door was suddenly swung open to reveal a slender feminine figure, shadowed against the bright glare of the living room.

"Hi Mr Martin, sorry, I didn't hear you come in."

"That's okay Rebecca. I know we're back a bit earlier than we said," he assured her, blinking against the sudden flood of light. Fortunately, his eyes adjusted quickly to the blaze, discerning the girl's soft doe-like eyes staring up at him from beneath the smooth wash of dark brown hair that she'd tied into a side braid over her left shoulder. Just nineteen, she had a long, sweet face and a petite yet shapely form that was clad in tight blue jeans and a pink floral T-shirt that ended just above her flat navel. "Has Alex been behaving himself?"

"Oh, he's been just wonderful. Little tyke hasn't made a peep since I put him down." Smiling up at him, she stepped back to let him pass into the flat's living room.

Neither spartan nor lavish, the furnishings were mainly teak and pine, equally as decorative as they were functional, as well as a wide three-person sofa of supple black leather that had been pressed against the wall and a Sony DVD player and 32' television that were mounted on the opposite wall. As he'd feared, the film *Twilight* was playing on the flat screen.

"So, how was the party? Did you have a good time?"

"Boring really. In fact, we were kicked out," he said, barely able to keep the wide grin at bay as he recalled Scarlet's venomous, jilted glare. He would probably pay merry hell for it on Monday, however. Scarlet always loved to play games and Alice had thrown a fine challenge her way tonight.

She may have won the battle, but he was sure the war had only just begun.

Plainly befuddled, Rebecca's eyebrow arched at his comment and for a moment he thought she would press him for further details, but the kettle began to whistle, and he heard Alice shout out a greeting to the girl. As she turned to reply, he took the opportunity to slip past and crossed the room in six quick strides before going through the open doorway leading to the bath and bedrooms. Taking care not to make a sound as he moved down the shadowy antechamber, he crept past the connecting bathroom and master bedroom before coming to the infant's room. Pushing the door ajar, just far enough for him to squeeze through, he stepped cautiously into the gloom beyond. A blue nightlight bathed the interior in a low gloom, illuminating the Star Wars cartoon wallpaper and providing just enough light for him to trek a route around the dozens of toys that lay scattered across the floor.

Sleeping peacefully in his cot, the infant Alexander never stirred as his father approached. If it had not been for his stormy grey-blue eyes and thick dark brown hair, the boy would have been the spitting image of his father and the sight of him curled around his favourite stuffed puppy brought a smile to Richard's face. Given their tenuous financial state, many of their friends and relatives had been surprised by his and Alice's decision to go through with the unexpected pregnancy. But Alice had always wanted to be a mother, and as there was simply no way of telling when the economy would heal, be it ten years or even a hundred. Life was just too short to turn down the blessing life handed them, and they had never been happier since little Alex came into their lives.

Bending forward, he placed a gentle kiss on the child's brow before drawing back and retreating from the room, gently pulling the door shut as he went.

Knowing he should go and pay Rebecca for her help but too eager to get out of his suit, he entered the master bedroom and flicked the light switch before casually shrugging off his jacket. Hurling it across the bed, he'd just begun fingering his tie when there was a sudden knock at the door and he turned around to see Rebecca standing in the doorway, with a sheepish look on her face and her *Twilight* DVD case in hand. Concern stabbed his heart with an icy dagger.

"Hey…Mr Martin, I'm sorry to interrupt you but I'm setting off now and well…my dad's gone away for a couple of days and before he left, he managed to screw up our laptop. I hate to ask, but he'll be home tomorrow and if he comes back to find it broken, he'll just blame me and force me to buy a new one, so…if it's not too much trouble, could you… well um-" The words were spilling from her in a tide of emotion and she looked on the verge of tears.

Richard gave her a reassuring smile. "Of course I can. You go on home and I'll be up to take a look in a minute."

"You will! Oh, thank you Mr Martin; I really appreciate this." Visibly relaxing, she turned on her heel and headed back through to the living room, leaving Richard alone with his thoughts and a quickly mounting temper.

"That rat bastard."

Though they lived on the floor above, he had only met Rebecca's father on one or two occasions, but each had left a lasting impression. Unlike his daughter, Derik Blaire was squat, heavy-shouldered, and prone to violent outbursts. Once happily married and a carrier squaddie, he'd been cashiered after getting drunk and striking an NCO whilst off duty, but still in uniform. A court-martial found him guilty of insubordination, behaviour unbecoming, and wilfully striking a non-commissioned officer. He'd lost his pension and been sentenced to confinement for three years before receiving a dishonourable discharge. In the months after his release, he was dismissed from six occupations before apparently abandoning the search for work. His wife, tired of his bullshit, left him for a younger man and moved up to Yorkshire to escape his continued harassment, leaving their daughter with her growingly aggressive and substance dependent father.

Richard was reluctant to ask about the pair's main source of income. He knew Rebecca worked part-time in a shop over in the Quays, as well as babysitting for them and a few other families in the building. However, that could hardly cover the costs of living, so he was sure there had to be more there than just met the eye.

Loosening his necktie enough to pull it over his head, he hurled the cloth across the bed to join his jacket before starting upon his black shirt but then thought better of it. He and Alice would be going to bed soon enough. There was no point dirtying fresh clothes. Even so, a stab of old vanities caused him to pause before his wife's standing mirror. Tall, clean-shaven, and relatively comely, he had deep blue eyes and medium length raven hair that framed a sharp jaw. Though only thirty-seven, his hair had been salted with a streak of silver, but Alice assured him it made him appear distinguished; he just prayed it didn't foretell his going bald.

Deciding he needed a drink, Richard moved on to the kitchen to find Alice already leaning against the fridge and sipping a steaming cup of tea, waiting for him. A half glass of wine sat on the counter beside her.

"How's Alex?" she asked, setting the cup down on the side and crossing her arms over her waist as he reached for the wine.

"Sleeping peacefully, thank God, and if we're lucky, he'll stay that way till morning. I swear that kid has a set of lungs on him that could wake the dead." Watching her carefully, he brought the glass to his lips and drained it in one swig. It tasted bitter, and he openly shuddered in disgust.

Alice, however, paid no mind to his displeasure. A few stray strands came loose from her thick mane to hang over her eyes, but she brushed them back into place without taking her gaze off him. "So, are you going to help her?"

"Of course I am."

She gave an approving nod. "It's shameful the way he treats her. The sooner she moves out of there, the better." They'd often heard Rebecca talk about moving out, going to live with friends or whatever boy teased her heart. Sometimes she even mentioned renting a little place of her own. However, she never seemed to be able to find enough money and after a few weeks, she'd lose her enthusiasm for the idea until the next time her father lost his temper and threw something at her. "Though I think she will miss you, Richard."

The remark caught him by surprise, and he coughed so hard the wine in his belly almost repeated on him. "Me? I have no idea what you mean, Love."

A sly smile lit up Alice's features and her throaty voice developed a noticeably playful tone. "How could you miss it? She's got a crush on you, Richard," she chuckled. "You're clueless. She watches your every move and smiles whenever she sees you. If she knows you're home, the poor girl gets dolled up just so you'll say she's pretty. And you know, I can't say that I'm not a little jealous." Stepping forward, she took the glass from his hand and placed it on the counter before closing the gap between them, her finger tracing invisible symbols over his chest. "She really is quite beautiful, isn't she?"

Richard's throat ran dry. Was she serious? Was she baiting him, or just stating a fact? Alice had always been blunt, and nobody could deny that Rebecca was certainly very pretty, but how could he agree with her without inadvertently risking her wrath? "Alice, I-"

Her lips silenced him as she suddenly went up onto the tips of her toes, their mouths crashing together in a devouring embrace as her hands moved to encircle his neck. Fierce and demanding, she held nothing back and quickly took the kiss deeper, the passion of it setting a fire in his flesh as her slick tongue invaded the moist warmth of his mouth to meet his own in a feverish dance. He felt his trousers growing tight as his cock sprang to life, powerless to resist his wife's errant ministrations as she drew him against her, one long shapely leg rising, curling around him.

His heart hammered in his chest as he wound his arms around her waist, drawing her closer. Her full breasts pressed against his chest, pebbled nipples poking through the satin like diamonds, and he could feel the heat of her desire against his thigh. His hands, so large upon her tiny frame, trailed down her spine to seize her buttocks, causing her to gasp into the kiss as he pulled her against his hard arousal. It had been so long, he needed her. Now, atop the counter, against the fridge, on the floor, he didn't care. He just had to have her...

"She really is quite beautiful, isn't she?" Her words echoed in his ears, sending a hot shiver down his spine as an image of Rebecca appeared before his eyes. She was arching in pleasure, locked in his arms, whimpering softly as he tasted the hollow of her throat. It was only a momentary lapse, but the mental image was enough to make him jump back, breaking the embrace.

Flushed and breathless, Alice almost lost her balance, and she flashed him an insidious look that both chilled and enflamed his ardour. "What's wrong?"

Fighting to catch his breath, Richard couldn't meet her gaze as guilt's cold fist turned his innards to ice. "We ca-can't do this now. I promised to help Rebecca; her father will be home tomorrow. If I don't go now, it'll be too late."

For a moment she looked as if she were about to protest, but she had always been fond of the girl and after a moment her face softened. She gave a short, defeated nod before turning away. "Fine, just don't be too long."

Her frosty tone was as much a dismissal as a slap in the face, yet as he departed the kitchen, he distinctly heard her declare, "I'll be waiting." The words were rich with promise, and he didn't know whether to cheer or weep.

Chapter Three

He knocked three times and then waited as the sound echoed nine times off the tower's inner walls. The air was thick with the sickly-sweet reek of drugs and somewhere a couple were shouting, their thunderous curses echoing through the walls like clangs on a bell. However, he was too distracted by the painful ache in his groin to take much notice. Digging his hand into his pocket, he tried to relocate his still swollen erection, but the trousers were barely large enough for him to thrust himself down the right leg. The inner pent-up agony persisted, nonetheless.

Shifting uncomfortably, he raised his hand to knock again, only to hear the *click* of the lock's inner mechanics unlocking before the door swung inward to reveal a vision of such beauty that Richard's breath caught, his engorged flesh growing ever more painful. Gone were her tight blue jeans and pink floral top. Instead, Rebeca had changed into a lacy, black robe that was tied around her narrow waist and barely covered her pale ivory thighs. She had also taken her hair out of its braid so that it cascaded down her back in a tangle of lustrous dark curls and framed her soft features.

She lit up at the sight of him. "Oh Mr Martin, thank God, I was starting to worry you weren't coming."

Once again, Alice's words echoed in his ears and Richard felt the heat rising in his cheeks as he realised he was staring. Flashing a hollow smile and praying she wouldn't notice the bulge straining against his right trouser leg, he said, "Rebecca, how many times have I asked you to call me Richard? Mr Martin makes me sound like some whining old geezer."

"Well, you are an old man, Mr Martin." Giggling playfully, she stepped aside to let him enter. "Would you like something to drink? Tea? Coffee?"

"Ahh…tea, milk and two sugars please and, *thanks*," he said, his voice dripping with sarcasm at the joke as he moved into the flat. The layout was almost identical to that of his and Alice's and he quickly moved down the hall into the Blaire's living room. With dim, off-cream walls and filled only by a small jumble of cheap mismatched furniture, it looked larger than it actually was.

A grubby old grey and blue denim sofa faced an even more ancient Panasonic television that had been mounted upon a near modern looking glass and steel stand that was certainly more functional than decorative. There was a single, three-tiered, mahogany veneer, bookcase, its shelves sagging under a dozen piles of dog-eared military and spy fiction paperbacks, a ceramic bowl atop a walnut look-alike end table under the window, as well as a massive opening night poster from the 80's hit-movie *Predator* that had been framed and hung on a wall. At the back of the room, a tall display case of solid teak stood in stark contrast to the items of veneered plywood scattered around it and held an impressive collection of Rebecca's swimming trophies. From a young age, the girl had been an avid swimmer and had even gone on to represent Gloucester in three county events, but after her parents' divorce, she had lost much of her enthusiasm for the sport. Now she rarely went more than once or twice a month.

The computer desk stood opposite the display case, the laptop already open and booting up. It was an ancient HP that hadn't been updated beyond Window's *Vista*. Sitting on the threadbare ottoman that the Blaire's employed as a chair and grimacing at the uncomfortable sensation in his semi-hard manhood, he logged into Rebecca's account and was immediately confronted by the problem as a virus conjured up an obviously falsified police lockdown. He tapped a few select keys, but to no effect. Next, he tried to open the start menu, but the virus brought up a warning box and cancelled the command. Finally, he logged out and entered Derik's account. The result was the same.

After a moment, Rebecca entered with his tea and placed it on an old *Top Gear* magazine lying beside the laptop. "Any luck?"

"Does this happen every time you log on?"

"Yes. It's been like this now for two days," she replied, her voice trembling as she peered far enough over his shoulder for him to taste her scent, reminding him of the first breath of spring. The scent steeled his length. "Can you fix it?"

Richard didn't answer. Instead, he pressed down on the power button until the screen went blank. Restarting the machine, he quickly switched to safe mode before letting it load up. Again, logging into the girl's profile, he waited a moment to make sure it didn't change again before going into its control panel and initiating a system restore to the pre-set point. It was a pretty routine trick that would work 99 times out of a 100. However, when he logged on for the third time, the scowling face of the law immediately opposed him.

"It might take a while."

Repeating the process of placing it in safe mode, he then filed through the recent system downloads and found that there were more than two hundred from the past thirty-six hours. He deleted them all, sipping his tea and cursing under his breath every time one or a dozen would randomly regenerate. When all of them were finally put down for good, he restarted the laptop and was finally met by Rebecca's normal background of a 'Hello Kitty' poster.

Exhaling a long breath, he gratefully pushed away from the desk and stretched his legs out to relieve the cramp building in his knees. It felt like he'd been at the desk for hours, but his tea was still lukewarm, so it couldn't have been any more than twenty minutes.

Throwing one leg over and around the ottoman, he twisted to face the sofa where Rebecca was now reclining, watching some cheesy Jennifer Aniston rom-com that was playing on ITV2 whilst eating from a carton of ice cream. The sight of her soft pink lips wrapped around the spoon sent a hot pulse straight down his spine and he heard her moan in delight, her soft brown eyes falling closed as she savoured its sweetness…

"There you go Rebecca, all done."

"Really!" Startled out of her trance, her head whirled to face him and as she shifted, the lace of her gown moved with her, flashing him a momentary glimpse of her soft ivory bosom. "Ohhh…thank you, thank you, Mr Martin!"

"You're welcome, Rebecca." It was time to go; he knew it as well as he knew the desire stirring in his loins. And yet he could not will his legs to move. "But you should really consider updating your security, or perhaps switching to a more secure browser."

"I know we do. I keep telling Dad, but he just ignores me. He thinks it will cost too much money. Ohhh…thank you so much Mr Martin, I don't know what I would have done without you." Then, almost giddy and still clutching her carton of ice cream, she sprang up from her seat and raced across the room to throw her arms around him in a tight hug. The embrace caught Richard off guard, and he could do little more than bask in the feeling of her young body pressed against him. He could feel her breath on his neck, hot as a furnace and tickling his every weak spot as the sweetness of her scent filled his every breath, causing a fog to descend upon his mind.

Time seemed to slip away. He couldn't say for how long she clung to him, yet when she finally broke the embrace, he felt light-headed and she couldn't meet his gaze. A blush touched her cheeks pink, and she quickly stepped back. He should go now. This was his chance, before things got even more complicated; all he had to do was politely say goodbye, leave, and then everything would be fine…

Yet the moment came and went, and the silence hung between them as a heavy iron collar, binding them to each other.

"You're eating ice cream, what flavour?" he finally asked, desperate for anything that might ease the tension.

Rebecca, however, seemed to have forgotten all about the carton and it was only when she looked down and saw it there that she realised icy drops of condensation were running off her fingers. "Ohhh…it is Tesco's Cherrylicious." She had such a sweet voice. Why hadn't he ever noticed it before? "Would you like some?"

Damn, he had always had a weakness for cherries. He knew he shouldn't, yet when she offered him the spoon, its head filled with a blend of fluffy white vanilla and thick gooey cherry, he couldn't resist and obediently opened his mouth to accept the sweet treat. The taste of it flooded his senses, as deliciously bitter as it was sweet, and he swallowed it all greedily. Yet as she pulled the spoon away, a single creamy drop escaped the corner of his mouth and ran wetly down his chin. He moved to brush it aside, but Rebecca's spoon was quicker, and she scooped up the droplet before bringing it to her own lips.

"Mmm…delicious," she moaned, and he realised it wasn't the ice cream's bitter-sweet flavour she had tasted, but his own. Seeming to sense his scrutiny, she suddenly stilled, and when their eyes met, they both knew the truth.

Heart pounding, he reached out and took the utensil from her before hurling it aside with a flick of his wrist. Then they came together, and he could feel his head spinning as their lips met. Rebecca didn't hesitate; the ice cream carton was gone, discarded. He knew not where or when, and she was upon him, straddling his waist. Wrapping her arms around his neck, she kissed him hungrily, her lips parting and her small tongue pressing against his lips, demanding entry.

Richard knew he should stop this before things went too far, but his body was acting on its own and his mouth opened to accept her, passionately returning the kiss as his hands seized her backside and crushed her to him. *She tastes like…cherries.*

Surrendering to the moment, a low growl rumbled through him as he lost himself in the intoxicating sweetness of her lips. He could feel her breasts pressing against him as her tongue ran wild within his mouth, brushing over his teeth and tickling the roof of his orifice. She let out a small moan as his tongue slipped over hers and hotly twirled around the probing muscle, pressing it back into the warmth of her mouth. All too aware of his fully engorged arousal straining for release from its tight confines, he used his hold on her buttocks to draw her closer, letting her feel the effect she was having on him as their tongues danced. Whimpering with pleasure, Rebecca eagerly responded by rocking her hips against his own and a hot shiver ran down his spine as he felt the damp heat of her desire through the mesh of garments.

Only when his breath was exhausted, and the need for air utterly dire, did he break the kiss. Yet drunk on her sweetness, he couldn't stop; grabbing deep ragged breaths, he swooped down and began to nip a trail of fire from the sensitive spot just under her ear, down the soft slope of her neck, and to the exposed crook of her shoulder. Gasping hotly in a mixture of pleasure and pain at every tiny subtle bite, Rebecca tilted her head back, exposing more skin for him to kiss as her fingers tangled in his hair, a ragged moan escaping her as his tongue traced the ridge of her collarbone.

Richard didn't care that he was leaving marks, that the girl's neck was red and glistening; he couldn't stop, couldn't get enough. He was addicted to her taste, her scent, the softness of her skin, and even the very feel of her writhing against him drove him wild; but it wasn't enough.

Tight and firm, her lace covered buttocks filled his hands nicely and he couldn't resist squeezing the luscious mounds, making the beauty moan, before trailing his hands up along her sides, mentally mapping the sensual curves before hooking a finger over the robe's belt. With a quick tug, the tie came undone, and the garment fell open. Keeping one hand locked to her narrow waist, the other slid beneath the folds of the robe to explore the previously hidden delights. Softer than silk but hot to the touch, her skin trembled at his lightest contact and he ran his fingers teasingly over the bumps of her ribs before coming to her bosom.

His hand moulded to her left breast, eager digits kneading the soft, supple flesh whilst his thumb and forefinger rolled the pebbled nipple. Thrilled by his touch, she arched her back, pressing her cleavage further into his palm, and moaned in utter wonder as he trailed his tongue along her collarbone in small gentle kisses, soothing the bite marks, her fingers tugging at his hair each time his thumb playfully squeezed her pert bud.

"Oh Mr Martin…mmm…yessss…*harder*!" she gasped, her breathing ragged with barely suppressed moans, before bowing her head and plunging her tongue into his ear, arousing him further.

His cock jumping at the strange sensation, Richard growled before releasing his hold on her breast and rearing backwards, ceasing his attentions to her neck, drawing an all too audible whimper of protest from Rebecca. Paying no mind to her discontent, he reached up with both hands and pushed the robe off her shoulders and down her arms, leaving her flawless ivory skin naked to his eyes, except for a matching thong of black lace. He wantonly devoured the sight of her near naked beauty. Lithe and willowy, she had a swimmer's body and though he was accustomed to the sight of her flat stomach and long shapely legs, it was as if he were seeing her for the first time. Full and firm, her tear-drop shaped breasts rose and fell with her every breath. Their milky complexion contrasted perfectly with her dusky pink nipples.

"I know they're…not very big," admitted Rebecca, her voice flat and barely above a whisper, drawing his attention up to her face as she disentangled her fingers from his hair to cross her arms over her chest. She couldn't meet his gaze and all the confidence was leeching from her features to leave an unmistakable mask of doubt, perhaps even fear; fear that he might find her unsatisfactory or repulsive.

The very idea filled him with such sour emotion that he was almost overwhelmed by the urge to crush her to him and promise her she was beautiful. Instead, he raised his hand to her wrists and gently lowered her arms. "No Rebecca, they're perfect; you're perfect."

She looked at him in alarm, her eyes misty with tears, yet before she could speak, his lips touched hers in a kiss. It was sweet and tender, and she didn't resist. When he pulled away, she tried to follow, but he swooped down and took her right nipple between his lips, making her gasp in pleasure. She arched into his touch, giving him easier access to her ample cleavage as his tongue playfully circled her nipple, drawing tantalising rings of fire around the stiff bud before sensually grazing it with his teeth.

"Ohhh…Mr Martin!" she moaned; he could feel her rocking earnestly against the bulge of his arousal. Her small hands moved to claw at his head, seizing great clumps of his raven locks before running down his neck and roaming the broad plane of his shoulders and back, his muscles bunching and contracting at the feel of her nails scraping through the thin cotton of his shirt. Shivering in a mix of pleasure and agony at her sharp touch, his hand moved back up to roughly knead her neglected breast while his lips continued their assault. No longer teasing, he began to suckle ravenously, his tongue skilfully flicking across her nipple while the rough pad of his thumb massaged its twin, enjoying the way she responded to his every touch.

No match for such an onslaught, Rebecca's head tipped back. She uttered a torrent of delightful sounds as she basked in the sensations he was stirring within her. Moaning and writhing against the trapped bulge of his arousal, her hands fumbled with the buttons of his shirt, her digits clumsy from her inexperience and desperation to rid him of the garment. When the last popped free, the shirt fell open and her hand moved down between their bodies, cupping the weight of his cock through his trousers.

"So-so big…" she gasped out hotly and he couldn't help uttering a low moan against her breast at the feeling of her fingers closing around him, her palm jerking up and down as she massaged his length. "Ooh God; please…take me to bed, Mr Martin!"

With his mind fogged by lust, Richard couldn't resist her and released her breast before seizing her buttocks with both hands and standing up from the ottoman. Squealing with delight, Rebecca crossed her legs over his waist and wrapped her arms securely around his neck, effectively clinging to him for dear life as he hoisted her up and carried her out of the living room and into the darkened hallway. Though this was the first time he'd been in this part of the Blaire's flat, as its layout was identical to that of his own, it was easy for him to navigate the gloom of the narrow antechamber towards the minor bedroom at its end, which he guessed was Rebecca's. He was tempted to try for the handle, but the feeling of Rebecca's lips on his neck persuaded him there was no time. One good kick was all he needed to have the door swing open.

Chapter Four

Rebecca's room was bright and vibrant, with pale blue wallpaper and polished pine furnishings. Framed posters of various animals hung on the walls, as well as a wall-mounted *Sony* combi, LCD television and DVD player, and a divan double bed that dominated one corner of the room. Approaching the side of the bed, he dropped her unceremoniously upon the divan, causing the girl to squeal with alarm, before stepping back and shrugging off his shirt. As the garment pooled around his feet, he felt goosebumps erupting over his arms as the chilly air touched his skin. Despite the cold, the ache in his groin had grown almost unbearable, and he quickly stepped out of his shoes and socks before pushing both his trousers and boxers down his legs, sighing with relief as his painfully stiff erection burst free of its confines.

Rebecca could only gasp, her big doe eyes shamelessly drinking in the sight of his masculinity before a hungry smile turned her lips. Feeling the heat of her gaze lingering upon him, Richard couldn't resist smirking before moving to join her on the black sheets. Relishing the image of her spread out beneath him, his eyes fixed on his last obstacle. Reaching out, he hooked his fingers under the hem of her panties, now visibly damp and glistening with dew, and dragged the sodden garment down her legs, leaving her completely exposed to his ravenous gaze.

Visibly trembling, Rebecca opened her legs, inviting him to continue. His mouth watering at the sight of her sex, he tossed the garment aside before leaning forward, drawn by the heady scent of her arousal, to hover above her folds.

"Mr Martin?" Her breath was shaky with need and impatience, as she watched him. "What are you do-ohhh!" The words fell into a long moan as his mouth descended upon her.

Plunged into a world of sensory delights, he thrust his tongue into her molten depths, stroking her plush inner-walls. She had a spiced, tangy flavour, and he was immediately addicted.

"Mmm…that feels so good…Mr Martin…" gasped Rebecca, her sweet voice breathless with pleasure as his tongue explored her channel. Savouring the taste of her, Richard held nothing back and ate her greedily. His tongue lapped and twirled, drawing a maze of intricate patterns across her inner walls before suddenly withdrawing between his jaws, only to plunge deeper into her centre.

Her hips jumped against him and he glanced up to see her head rolling back, her eyes closed and mouth open in a long moan. Grinning inwardly at the look of pleasure etched upon her features, he slid her legs over his shoulders before seizing her buttocks, supporting her weight easily, and drawing her closer while swirling his tongue around the deepest part of her, making her buck and cry with pleasure.

"Ohhhhhhhh!!!" she moaned before seizing white knuckled handfuls of the sheets, her hips rolling wantonly against his mouth, demanding more.

"Mmm…you're delicious," he murmured against her flesh, rolling his tongue to the rhythm of her body and feeling his cock jump as her sounds of pleasure sent a pulse of electrified excitement coursing through his nerves. Absorbing everything he was doing to her, Rebecca could only writhe and moan as her senses were overloaded and he could feel the mounting tension within her as she approached her heavenly summit.

Far from finished with her, however, Richard withdrew his tongue from her heat and drew it gently up her folds to teasingly circle her clitoris before closing his mouth over the beauty's swollen bud, a grin crossing his thin lips at her sudden cry of rapture.

"Ohhh-shit-yesss!" she shrieked, her big brown eyes dark with lust, widening to the size of saucers as his lips wrapped around the tiny bud and drew it into the heat of his mouth, suckling it. When his tongue flicked it, slender fingers tangled in his hair, dragging him closer as her hips bucked wildly against his orifice. "Ugh-right there…don't stop-ahhh-yes, yes, yes, YES!"

He focused all his attention on that small bundle of nerves, delighting in her cries of ecstasy while skilfully swirling his tongue over and around, switching randomly between sharp licks and teasing rolls again and again; keeping her purposefully on edge as the sweet oblivion welled up within her. Clearly unprepared for the rush of sensations, Rebecca could do little more than gasp and pant and cry out in delight, her fingers tugging urgently at his hair whilst her hips bucked and rolled beneath his sinfully wicked motions.

And then, suddenly, the truth of his situation caught up to him.

Ohhh God...*what the hell am I doing!* Richard thought, yet all the while unable to resist admiring the way her body danced as his tongue expertly jabbed at her clit, his firm grip holding her in check even as she strained for more. This wasn't him. Richard Martin never cheated; he was a loyal husband who loved his wife. He didn't do things like this, he couldn't, it wasn't right...

Desperately, he tried to conjure up a vision of Alice but the image of her seemed to linger just out of memory, dancing before his gaze within a haze of smoke and mist before a sharp, agonising pain shot along the length of his erection, reminding him of his own pressing need. Beaten, his body acted on its own accord and he caught the bundle of nerves between his teeth while humming a low rumbling *"Mmm..."*

"Ohhh right there...right there-oh God-ughhh I'm cumming...oh God-oh God-ohhh goooohhhhhhhhh!!!" Rebecca cried, losing all control, deliriously thrashing her head and arching off the sheets; her whole body trembling with the force of the climax ripping through her. Unchecked, Richard worked her down from the heights before gently lowering her onto the bed, her eyes falling shut as she basked in the wondrous aftermath. This was his chance. It wasn't too late. All he had to do was get dressed and leave, now.

Yet his brain was fogged, and his limbs wouldn't move. He was standing on the bank of the *Rubicon*. Should he cross its depths, there would be no turning back, he would be lost, adrift in purgatory, and everything he loved would be at stake, forfeit. If Alice were to learn of it, their marriage would be over, his son would grow up to despise him, friends and family would shun him like a stray dog. And yet, could he live with himself if he didn't, knowing he'd come this far only to turn away, and always wondering what it would have been like?

But then the decision was taken out of his hands. Flushed and panting, Rebecca's eyes fluttered open, and she looked up at him dreamily. "Come on, come on…don't stop now. Ohhh God, I'm so hot. Please fuck me, Mr Martin! I need you to fuck me…"

How could he resist?

Alea iacta est.

Crawling up the length of her body, covering her slender frame as he rose above her and settled between her splayed legs. He didn't worry about a condom; he knew Rebecca had been on the pill since her sixteenth birthday. Alice had taken her to the hospital to get a prescription. Seeing the lust burning in those innocent doe eyes, the last of his resistance melted away, and he plunged into her molten core.

"Ohhh," Rebecca moaned at the sudden invasion, her eyes widening and head rolling back into the mess of tangled sheets as he entered her, burrowing inside bit-by-bit, filling her completely.

"Ughhh…" Richard groaned once he was completely embedded within her liquid heat, almost losing himself in the feeling of inner walls stretching and wrapping around his engorged flesh. The urge to move was so overwhelming that it took every bit of his willpower to remain still, relishing the feel of her tight embrace as he drew in deep ragged breaths and waited for her to adjust to his size. He'd known she wasn't a virgin for some time; but she was still so tight and though he was far from huge, he must have been considerably larger than what she was accustomed to. The realisation sent a delightful thrill down his spine, and his cock twitched.

"Ahhh…" cried the girl, her inner muscles tensing around him so tightly that he was afraid he'd hurt her and began to withdraw. "No! Don't stop. Do it again…."

His cock throbbed dangerously at her words and the slick snugness of her walls made him pant as he began to rock his hips. He moved in small rowing motions, delighting in the friction between their bodies. Arching beneath him as he rolled his hips, Rebecca seized his buttocks with both hands, her fingernails digging into his flesh before dragging trails of fire up his lower back as her legs wrapped around his flanks, crossing at the ankles, and urging him to go deeper while rocking urgently against his gentle motions.

"Ooohhhh God! Give it to me Mr Martin…I want it…I want it…ahhhhh-yes-yesss" Her words fell into an endless stream of moans and gasps as he drew back until just the bulbous head remained encased within her, before thrusting back into her hard and fast. She jumped at his intrusion, her delicate insides rippling and convulsing around his hard length, trying to draw him deeper. Enjoying the feel of her squirming beneath him, he repeated the motion, again and again, building a steady rhythm that had him delving deeper with every thrust. He'd meant to be slow and gentle, to take it easy on her, but she had proved his undoing in that first delicious instant.

He felt maddened, bewitched, and so utterly out of control. Lust burned hot and molten through his veins, and just the sight of her writhing beneath him, wantonly begging for more, was nearly too much for him to bear. Suddenly there was nothing gentle in his motions, just a desperate, unyielding need.

"Ughhh…so-so tight," he growled; his voice choked with pleasure as he thrust back inside her plush passage, filling her completely, the feeling of her inner walls squeezing his returning flesh almost pitching him over the edge and he knew he wouldn't last much longer. It had been over a month since he and Alice last had sex, and the torment of the night's games had left his cock so sensitised he thought it might burst at any moment. *But not yet. Not yet!*

"Ohhh fuck…your dick feels so good…oh-oh-ohhh…don't stop…don't stop!" cried Rebecca, eagerly meeting every one of his downward strokes with an upward roll of her hips, her nails clawing madly at his back each time his pelvis grazed her clit. He was certain she was leaving marks, but at this point, it was hard to be concerned about anything, even of discovery by his loving wife, who was waiting for him in the flat below them.

"Mmm…So is this what you want, Rebecca?" Fighting to ignore the rush of pleasure creeping up his spine as he plunged into the deepest parts of the beauty, Richard held nothing back, hastening his thrusts until the bed beneath them seemed to be rocking to their wild rhythm. The sound of it all was music to his ears; the squeaking of bedsprings, the wet slapping of flesh on flesh and, of course, Rebecca's overwhelmed moans.

"Yes, yes…it was always you…I've always wanted you, Mr Martin…Oh God! Feels so good, fuck me harder…HARDER!" A cry of rapturous delight tore from her lips as his hips snapped in deep, long strokes that made her spine curl and her breasts bounce. Like him, she was nearing her peak. He could feel the balls of her feet beating against his arse, urging him to push her over that summit she so desperately yearned to reach.

Somewhere, buried deep in the depths of his subconscious, a part of him dreaded that inevitable conclusion, perhaps still hoping that this was all some wonderful, but monstrous nightmare and that his failure would banish this all away, like a foul odour on a great gust of wind. He might even have felt guilty for using the girl so thoughtlessly, had she not been writhing wantonly beneath him, meeting him thrust for thrust and begging for more. But he had come too far to stop now.

Feeling his release building, his sanity hanging by a thread; he reared back, his hands coming up to seize the swells of her buttocks, hoisting her off the sheets and pulling her firmly against him as he continued to thrust into her wildly. Inhaling sharply at this new angle, Rebecca's head rolled back in a voiceless cry and her hands fell away to brace against at the wall, searching desperately for some kind of purchase while doing her best to match his furious rhythm.

"Ah…ahhh-oh my God-oh my God-oh my God…I can't take it… it's too much…too big!" she shrieked, her fingers clawing at the walls and eyes wide with pure ecstasy. "Oh yes…yesssss…don't stop…I'm all yours Mr Martin…I've wanted your hard cock inside me for so long…you can fuck me whenever you want to…just don't stop…don't stop!"

The room was thick with the musky scent of sex. Grunting as he surged inside her, Richard savoured the sight of her pleasure-drunk features as his hands, roughly kneading her tight young arse like dough, guided her motions in time with his own. Spurred on by her heated encouragements, and the wondrous feeling of her molten channel writhing around his sensitised organ, he slammed into her mercilessly. His back was afire and he could feel beads of sweat rolling down his brow as he thrust hard and fast between her silky thighs, working tirelessly to push them both off their approaching peaks, the tingling sensation down in the base of his spine warning him of his impending oblivion.

"Ohhhh God…I can feel it…I'm going to cum…. fuck me, fuck meeeeee!" Rebecca cried, racing towards another climax and sobbing with pleasure while thrashing her head from side to side. "Ohhh-yes-yes…I'm cummingaahhhhhhhh!" her voice dissolved into a shrill cry of pleasure, and her inner walls erupted, convulsing around his thick length in a wash of molten warmth as she rode the orgasm, quivering and bucking against him uncontrollably.

Richard groaned in primitive delight, teetering on the brink, watching avidly as she came undone before the feelings the girl was stirring finally proved too much and a thunderous roar burst from his jaws. Slamming into her one last time, he felt something deep inside his abdomen contract and pulse, and then there was only the fire coursing through his veins as he released his essence into her warmth.

Exhausted beyond measure, they collapsed together in a heap on the bed.

Breathing hard and trembling with miniature aftershocks, Richard had just enough sense left to roll off the beauty, withdrawing his softening arousal from her still vivacious channel. Whimpering at the feeling of emptiness, Rebecca curled into his flank, the feeling of her nestling against him, drawing a low moan from the exhausted man as all notion of time slipped away. For several long moments, he was content to just bask in the glow of a much-needed release. Sleep's warm embrace dragging him down to that peaceful abyss…

He jerked at the sensation of falling, shattering the spell and leaving him cold, naked, and very much awake.

I need a shower. It was a strange thought. He knew he should have felt guilty, afraid, and perhaps even sick to his stomach, but oddly, a sense of calm detachment seemed to have settled over him and all he could really think about was how clammy his skin felt as the sheen of sweat covering him began to dry. He felt movement against his arm and glanced over to see Rebecca sleeping peacefully beside him, with an arm draped over his front and her head resting peacefully on his shoulder. She was smiling contentedly.

Chapter Five

"I have to go." He had tried to say it softly, so as to avoid disturbing her entirely, but his throat was dry and what came out was a raspy parody of a voice. Her body quivered in surprise at the sound and her eyes fluttered open, glassy with unshed tears.

"But…but can't you stay with me tonight?"

"You know I can't." In truth, he would have liked nothing better than to stay with her, but he knew Alice would be growing worried and it wouldn't be long before she came looking for him. The thought of her finding them like this sent the first true shiver of fear down his spine, and with the idea of her barging through the door, dressed like Rambo and armed with enough firepower to orbit Schwarzenegger in mind, he gently pushed her aside and sat up. Rising to his feet, he quickly set about collecting the garments that were scattered across the floor. Yet his mind was only half on the task, and as a result, he had done up more than half of his shirt's buttons before realising two of them were in the wrong hole. Even so, he couldn't keep from cringing when the cloth touched his back. The skin there felt painfully raw and inflamed; he'd need to be careful Alice didn't see the marks for a couple of days.

Finally dressed, though appearing curiously dishevelled, he straightened up and was about to leave when he heard the rustle of bedsheets.

"Please…Richard, promise me this wasn't just a one-night stand," Rebecca called out and despite his better judgement, he glanced back and his heart nearly broke at the vision of her sitting there, desperately trying to hide her nakedness by clutching the soiled sheets to her chest, her ivory skin almost glowing and big doe eyes sparkling pleadingly. Even after such a thorough fucking, she was no less a vision of innocence and purity, the sweetest of temptations.

"We'll see," he said, trying to keep his voice flat and features stern, hiding the sudden stab of emotion in his chest. He left without a backwards glance, shutting the bedroom door firmly behind him, doing his best to ignore Rebecca's tearful sobs.

Here's a sneak peek…

She shrugged. "Then, what about her? Sex isn't a luxury, Dick. It's a necessity. The body needs it like it needs food and water. If you're not getting any at home, then you need to look for it elsewhere. If having a little on the side gets the urge out of your system just enjoy the adventure while it lasts."

"Spoken like a woman who's never been married."

Scarlet smirked triumphantly and gestured at him with another plump strawberry. "And who never wants to. Humans aren't monogamous by nature, so why should I be, just because society demands it? I'm a girl with needs who doesn't like to be tied down, and matrimony is one big leash, Dick, especially when there are so many men out there I haven't tried yet."

She dunked half the berry into the dip. "Besides, what good would telling her do? Cheaters say being honest is the right thing to do, but all they really want is to make themselves feel better about fucking up. She'll be happier not knowing."

"It's still wrong."

"How so? Is it wrong to grab a bite on the way home even though your wife is cooking dinner? No. You're hungry, so you eat. Why should sex be any different?" Her eyes then sparkled with mischief as she nibbled along the chocolate. "If it bothers you so much, just grow a pair and tell her. Or try for a three-way?"

"Now I know you're joking."

"Why not, it would certainly solve all your problems," she teased, stretching out one long graceful leg, the toe of her high-heel shoe, white to match her dress, brushing along his thigh and down his leg. "And it's certainly not adultery if your wife's banging her too."

"Except Alice would cut my balls off and wear them as earrings," he breathed, forcing himself to look into her eyes, refusing to look down, all too aware of the unobstructed view she was offering him. Sharon Stone couldn't have done it better herself.

Holding his gaze, she leant forward until they were almost nose to nose. "I don't know, from what I saw she's definitely full of surprises. It's always the up-tight ones that you've got to watch."

"Drop it Scarlet," he warned, gritting his teeth, his dick hard and tight and impossible to ignore.

"Am I right, Dick? I am, aren't I? Yeah, I bet she turns into a little nympho the moment her hair comes down." She dropped the plate of strawberries on the desk and reached out to finger his tie.

"Scarlet… I'm warning you." His throat was tight around the words as his heart pounded in his ears. Shit, he needed to get out of here. She was too close, he couldn't think, couldn't breathe, her damn perfume was fogging his head.

Damnit, why did she have to smell so good…

"Mmm… you know you're cute when you're flustered." She closed the gap, sliding off the desk and onto his lap so the weight of his cock was lodged against the crotch of her dress. "Come on Dick, don't be greedy, she'll love going down on your little babysitter while you fuck her doggyst-"

Her taunt died in a surprised gasp as he seized a fistful of her blonde hair.

Also Available … The Final Temptation

Age is just a number, and this collection of sinfully steamy age-gap romances will prove it...

The Lord of lust has done it again and in this anything but sweet, four book Box Set, full of forbidden Silver Foxes and sassy Cougars, he proves that age is no boundary to love, or lust.

A collection of hot and orgasmic stories by The Lord of Lust
Do you love hard men, strong women, sizzling chemistry and erotic scenes that make Fifty Shades of Grey look like five shades of beige?
Well, here you go…
7 Books, 7 hard and rugged men, 7 sizzling page turners that will have you devouring every word from start to finish…

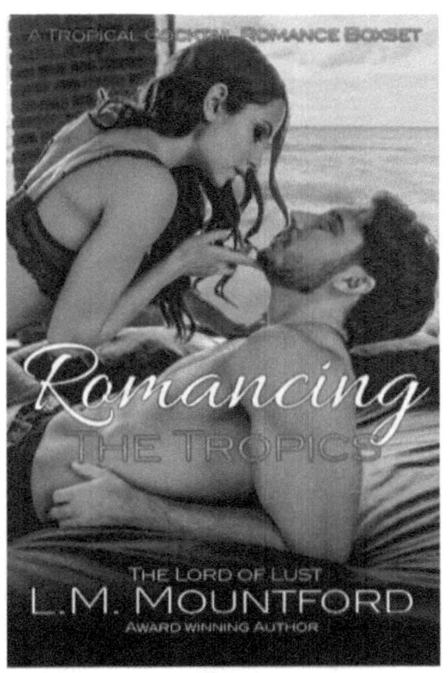

A Tropical Cocktail Boxset
Romance is in the air in this two book Holiday Romance boxset that is all about sun, sea and sex…
Tequila Sunset
Beneath The Sheets

The battle of the Species is about to rage, and only the true alpha will come out on top in the Lord of Lust hottest new duo boxset that sees vampires and werewolves lock tooth and claw…

To all the rest of the world, Elizabeth Clarke has it all.
A successful husband. A beautiful home. And now a son off to university. She is a perfect housewife with the perfect life.
It's a lie.
Her husband is a lying, drinking philanderer who hates her as much as she loathes him. Her home is beautiful, but empty, nothing more than a gilded cage to keep her trapped in a world she never wanted.
That is, until he came back into town.
Hugh Becket.
Her son's best friend. He's hot, young, and so forbidden.
Elizabeth knows she should stay away, but when the devil comes knocking on her door in the middle of the night, what's a poor neglected trophy wife to do?

He is my Hades

I'd played the role of a goddess, bound and chained for the service of mortals.

He freed me.

He freed me, unchained me and taken me to his underworld, his dark realm where he'd brought out all my forbidden and secret desires.

And now I'm his.

His attendant. His servant…

When Mina returns for her stepbrother's 21st birthday, she thinks her days of lusting after him are over. Caught up in the heat and passion of the moment, she is stunned to find them back in bed together; their feelings clearly far from resolved.

Haunted by her desire, Mina now has another problem… she must head down a path of lust and desire; torn between the dark delights of the handsome bad boy down the street and her adorable stepbrother who has always been there for her.

Can she confront the truth she has long tried to bury? How far will she go to save the one she wants, but knows she can never truly have?

As an underworld princess, daughter to the boss of mob bosses all along the east coast, Sophie's life was a gilded cage. A prison of gold and silk…
That is until Luke stepped into her life.
A scrapper from the back streets, who had risen from among the ranks to stand in her shadow.
Luke, her bodyguard, and her secret lover.
Their destinies were never meant to cross, but they had. It was impossible, forbidden, but they couldn't resist…
Now their one reckless night has become a desperate fight for their lives.

THE LORD OF LUST
L.M. MOUNTFORD

I know it's wrong to want my best friend's dad… but what about when his wife offers to share?
Tracey has known the Burtons practically all her life.
They're her best friend's parents.
When she was a little girl they took her on days out to the beach. But she's a woman now, and they have some very important lessons to teach her…

'I'm sorry Cassy, but you're just too boring for me,'
That was the story of Cassandra's life.
She was always that girl. The curvy plain jane. She was fine with it,
right up until her hot bad boy ex threw it in her face before walking out
of her life. Leaving her depressed and reeling, doubting everything
about herself and her future…
So her best friend has spirited her away to her family's Gibraltar Vila
for a little fun in the sun, some much needed girl time, and a whole lot
of boys.
There's just one problem.
David, her best friend's recently divorced dad also happens to be
staying at the villa. And he's no boy…

Sooner or later, the thirst always wins…
After a thousand years, Lucian had given up any interest in the world.
His only concern that night was finding his next drink, preferably from
a flavoursome twenty-something with loose morals and no
expectations. Then he saw her…
Kate is just a girl from the country, who came to the city with her
brother to find a life away from their parents' car crash. That is, until
the police came knocking on her door one morning and ripped her new
life apart.
Now she has nothing and no one, with only one on her mind…
When these worlds collide, and the things that go bump in the night
come calling, can these two mend the rifts in each other and give them
what they need?

Alex's life was circling the drain, and he was officially one step away from hitting rock bottom after finding his long-term girlfriend in bed with his biggest clients.

Then one morning an email arrives from the last person on earth he ever expected to hear from again.

Sarah Snow. His childhood friend, and the uncontested love of his life whom he hasn't seen since prom night.

And before he could say travel agent, he was boarding the first plane bound for Sydney, Australia, with nothing but his passport and an overnight bag.

He's no idea what he'll do or say when he finally reunites with the girl that broke his heart, but one thing's for sure…

He's not going home without her.

www.ingramcontent.com/pod-product-compliance
Lightning Source LLC
Chambersburg PA
CBHW031328060726
47590CB00003B/1365